THE MADCAP MYSTERY OF THE MISSING Liberty Bell

First Edition ©2009 Carole Marsh/Gallopade International/Peachtree City, GA
Current Edition ©August 2015
Ebook Edition ©2011
All rights reserved.
Manufactured in Peachtree City, GA

Carole Marsh Mysteries™ and its skull colophon are the property of Carole Marsh and
Gallopade International.

Published by Gallopade International/Carole Marsh Books. Printed in the United States
of America.

Managing Editor: Sherry Moss
Senior Editor: Aimee Holden
Assistant Editor: Susan Walworth
Cover Design: Vicki DeJoy
Cover Photo Credits: Photos.com
Picture Credits: Vicki DeJoy
Content Design and Illustrations: John Hanson

Gallopade International is introducing SAT words that kids need to know in
each new book that we publish. The SAT words are bold in the story. Look
for this special logo beside each word in the glossary. Happy Learning!

Gallopade is proud to be a member and supporter of these educational organizations
and associations:

American Booksellers Association
American Library Association
International Reading Association
National Association for Gifted Children
The National School Supply and Equipment Association
The National Council for the Social Studies
Museum Store Association
Association of Partners for Public Lands
Association of Booksellers for Children
Association for the Study of African American Life and History
National Alliance of Black School Educators

Once upon a time…

Hmm, kids keep asking me to write a mystery book. What shall I do?

Mimi

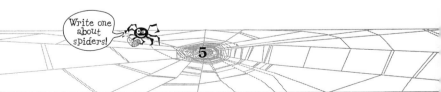

Write one about spiders!

Papa said …

Why don't you set the stories in real locations?

That's a great idea! And if I do that, I might as well choose real kids as characters in the stories! But which kids would I pick?

MIMI, PICK ME, PICK ME!

ME, TOO, MIMI, PICK ME, TOO!

Christina

Grant

Pick me!

You two really are characters, that's all I've got to say!

Yes you are! And, of course I choose you! But what should I write about?

national parks!

SCARY PLACES!

Famous Places!

FUN PLACES!

Disney World!

New York City!

Dracula's Castle

GRAND CANYON

On the *Mystery Girl* airplane ...

I can FLY US anywhere!

Or aboard the *Mimi!*

Take me to the Forbidden City!

Or by surfboard, rickshaw, motorbike, camel ...

All great ideas! I can put a lot of history, MYSTERY, legend, lore, and laughs in the books! We can use other boys and girls in the books. It will be educational and fun!

Good stuff!

9

And so, Mimi, Papa, Christina, and Grant took off aboard the *Mystery Girl* and America's National Mystery Book Series—where the adventure is real and so are the characters! —was born.

START YOUR ADVENTURE TODAY!

ABOUT THE CHARACTERS

Christina
Yother
Age 10

Grant
Yother
Age 7

Isabella
Vranesevich
Age 11

Hunter
Mercer
Age 11

1
HOT GHOSTS?

Christina glanced nervously at the photograph in her hand and scanned the crowd once more. Her grandmother Mimi pulled a pair of red, rhinestone-studded sunglasses from her purse and parked them on her face.

"Think you'll recognize him when you see him?" she asked.

"I hope so," Christina answered, as she eyed her reflection in Mimi's flashy shades. "You know kids our age can change a lot in a year!"

Mimi nodded in agreement. Christina had grown two inches and had gotten braces since she sent Hunter her picture at the beginning of the school year.

Christina wondered if Hunter would look different from the photograph he sent her. Their classes had joined in a pen pal project to learn more about kids in other cities. She wrote him about her home in Peachtree City, Georgia, and all the history and sights of nearby Atlanta. Hunter wrote her about his hometown of Philly. That's what he called Philadelphia, Pennsylvania, the birthplace of the United States. Through their letters, they had become good friends.

When Hunter invited Christina and her younger brother Grant to visit, she worried...Hunter liked her letters, but would he like her in person?

Mimi, also known as mystery writer Carole Marsh, was all for it. "I've been planning a historical mystery!" she had said excitedly. "That'll be a great place for research! Papa and I would love to take you!"

After they settled on going several days before July 4th, Papa had agreed to fly them in his little red and white plane, *Mystery Girl*. He warned that the heat might be sweltering. He was right.

"Where's Papa with those snow cones already?" Mimi asked, impatiently tapping her red, high heel shoe on the old brick path. "You stay here and keep watching for Hunter while I find Papa and something cool!"

Christina mopped her upper lip with the tail of her green cotton blouse and wished she'd worn her favorite pink tank top instead. Along the meandering paths of Old City, the historical heart of Philadelphia, she saw heat waves dancing above the hot brick like shimmering ghosts. She imagined how hot the Founding Fathers must have been when they walked these paths in their powdered wigs, breeches, and stockings. It must have been even worse for the women in their long dresses and layers and layers of petticoats.

Suddenly, Christina felt a searing pain in her neck. "Ouch!" she yelped.

Are the ghostly figures I daydreamed about trying to get my attention? Christina wondered.

2
TOO MANY Ns

A muffled snicker caused Christina to whirl around. It was Grant! Standing behind her on a bench, he was directing a sunbeam on her neck with his jumbo magnifying glass.

She grabbed for it and yelled, "Are you trying to catch my ponytail on fire!?"

Grant dodged, hopped off the bench, and wove through tourists like a snake on a busy highway. Christina chased in hot pursuit, her long, chestnut-colored hair slipping out of its ribbon and flying wildly around her face.

She caught Grant's shirt, but tripped on a loose brick. Both slid across sprinkler-soaked grass.

"Give me that magnifying glass!" she ordered, wrestling it from his hands.

"Don't forget Philadelphia's nickname," Grant said between giggles. "You can't hurt me! We're in the City of Brotherly Love!"

Christina stood and held the magnifying glass triumphantly in the air, but suddenly realized she was a mess. Bits of grass and mud clung to her shirt and arms. Her white shorts had a grass stain that even Mr. Clean® couldn't remove. And her hair stuck to her sweaty face like a spider web. She started to brush herself off when she felt a light tap on her shoulder.

"Christina, is that you?" a surprised voice asked.

Oh no! Christina's thoughts raced. *Please don't let it be him!* She turned, sheepishly. It was Hunter. He looked a lot like his picture—dark brown hair and big brown eyes.

"Wow!" Hunter said. "I knew you were interested in the Revolutionary War, but I didn't know you'd be fighting a battle!"

Christina's face was as red as Mimi's favorite hat. "Sorry I look this way," she stammered. "I had to take care of a little brother problem. It's great to finally meet you!"

She noticed Hunter had a girl with him. She had long brown hair and brown eyes. "You must be Hunter's neighbor, Isabella," Christina said.

"How did you know my name?" the girl asked shyly.

"Hunter told me about you in his letters," said Christina.

Mimi and Papa stormed toward them with sticky snow cone juice dripping off their hands. "You're not where I left you!" Mimi said sternly. "But I see you found Hunter!"

"My dad's waiting for us at the Liberty Bell Center," Hunter said.

Papa licked his snow cone to stop the drips from making sticky dots on his cowboy boots. "Let's go," he said. "I'm melting faster than this snow cone!"

Outside the Liberty Bell Center, a long rectangular building with glass walls, Christina was surprised to see Hunter walk up to a tall man dressed like an American Revolutionary War soldier. When he took the musket rifle off his shoulder and held out a big hand to Christina, she realized it was Hunter's dad.

"I feel like I know you already!" he said. "Hunter has talked about you all year."

Christina blushed when she remembered how awful she looked.

"I've got to take part in a historical re-enactment," he continued. "Hunter can show you around Old City."

After saying goodbye to Hunter's dad, they strolled down a long gallery filled with displays about the Liberty Bell and people who have fought for freedom around the world.

Suddenly, Hunter told Christina to close her eyes. "Keep 'em closed!" he warned, leading her through the gallery. "OK, now look."

Christina gasped. There it was, in all its old and cracked glory. Gleaming in the sunlight was the legendary Liberty Bell.

"The postage stamp doesn't do it justice!" Christina exclaimed.

"Too bad about the crack," Grant said sadly. "I read that they tried to put it in a cast."

Papa chuckled. "You should read more carefully, Grant," he said. "The original bell, made by Whitechapel Foundry in England, cracked the first time it was rung. Two foundry workers named Pass and Stow melted that bell and cast, or formed, a new one. People made fun of the way the second bell sounded, so Pass and Stow broke it up, melted it, and tried again. The third attempt is the one that became the Liberty Bell. Don't you see Pass and Stow's name on the bell?"

Hunter waved to an elderly man leaning on a cane.

"Who's that?" Christina asked.

"Another one of my neighbors, Mr. Whiddon," Hunter replied. "He was in World War II. He visits the Liberty Bell and remembers his buddies who died during the war. He always says that they died for what the bell represents. He's been chosen to tap the Liberty Bell on July 4th."

"Tap the bell?" Christina asked, confused.

"It's a special ceremony every July 4th," Hunter explained. "Because of the crack, the bell can't be rung, so it's gently tapped."

Mimi

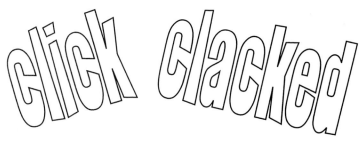

by them in her red high heels. "Did you read what's written on the bell?" she asked.

Grant craned his neck and squinted to read the raised letters: *Proclaim Liberty throughout all the land unto all the inhabitants thereof.*

"Hey, I remember reading that in Sunday school," he said.

"Yep," Mimi agreed.   "It's a Bible verse, *Leviticus 25:10.*"

Remembering the magnifying glass, Christina pulled it out and studied the bell. She rubbed her eyes and peered again. Hunter and Grant noticed her dumbfounded expression.

"Christina, are you okay?" Hunter asked.

"There are too many Ns!" she whispered.

An important discovery!

3
PENNY FOR YOUR THOUGHTS

"What gives, Tia?" Grant begged as they strolled out of Liberty Center.

"Yeah," Hunter said, "What has too many Ns?"

"The bell!" Christina answered.

"There are no Ns in bell," Grant said, rolling his eyes. "Even lousy spellers know that."

"You don't understand," Christina explained. "Pennsylvania is spelled P-E-N-N-S-Y-L-V-A-N-I-A with two Ns in Penn."

"Congratulations!" Hunter said and laughed. "You know how to spell my home state."

"No!" Christina said, annoyed. "Don't you get it? I read everything I could get my hands on about the Liberty Bell before we came here. When the bell was made, the makers spelled Pennsylvania P-E-N with only one N!'"

"Oh no!" Grant wailed as Christina's words sunk in. "Why does it always happen to us? We're like mystery magnets every time we take a trip with Mimi and Papa. And here we are, knee deep in another one. For once I'd like to be a plain old tourist like everyone else."

"Are you saying that what's hanging in Liberty Center is not the real Liberty Bell?" Hunter asked.

"That's exactly what I'm saying!" Christina said.

Isabella had been quiet as a mouse until now. "We should call 9-1-1," she said.

"We can't tell anyone, Isabella," Christina said, shaking her head matter-of-factly. "The bell is one of our greatest symbols of freedom. Without it, Independence Day wouldn't be much of a celebration. We just have to get to the bottom of this before July 4th!"

"That's only four days from now!" Isabella exclaimed.

Grant was suddenly distracted. "You smell a mystery, but I smell something delicious!" he said, sniffing the air.

The fragrant aroma of sizzling onions, peppers, and steak teased their taste buds.

"You've got a good nose," Hunter said. "That's another of Philadelphia's treasures, the cheesesteak."

The scrumptious smell tempted Papa, who was following behind them. "Who's hungry?" he asked.

Soon, they were chomping on sandwiches almost as long as their arms, and listening to a nearby fife and drum corps playing Revolutionary War tunes.

"Use your napkin, Grant," Christina mumbled with her mouth full. She laughed as Grant swiped at the strings of cheese hanging off his chin.

"So far, I love Philadelphia!" Grant said, rubbing his tummy.

Stuffed, they headed down Market Street for Franklin Court.

"Wanna see the Ghost House?" Hunter asked.

"Sure!" Grant exclaimed. "Ghosts don't scare me!"

"Meet you in a few!" Christina promised Mimi and Papa as she and Grant scampered behind Hunter and Isabella in anticipation.

Grant soon grew impatient. "I don't see anything!" he whined.

"It's right in front of you!" Hunter said, pointing to a metal frame outline of a house.

"Nothing's there," Christina said.

"Ever hear of Ben Franklin?" Isabella asked.

"Of course," Christina replied. "He's one of the Founding Fathers of our country and he helped write the Declaration of Independence."

"That's where his house used to be," Isabella said. "It was torn down in 1812."

"C'mon, you can see the foundation and the privy hole," Hunter said.

"The what?" Grant asked.

Christina whispered, "You know, the old-timey bathrooms people had before indoor plumbing."

"Oh," Grant said. "I guess I never thought of Ben Franklin having to use the bathroom."

The three sat down on a foundation stone of Franklin's house. "I wonder what old Ben would think about our little mystery?" Christina wondered aloud.

"Why don't you ask him?" Hunter said.

Christina looked up in surprise to see the familiar, white-haired Franklin. He peered at them through the little round glasses perched on the end of his nose.

"Penny for your thoughts," Franklin said, tossing a coin that Grant eagerly hopped up to catch.

"Just wondering what you'd think if the Liberty Bell went missing," Christina said.

"I've heard that old bell ring many times," Franklin said. "Some people complained that it rang too much. They even rang it when I went to England to address colonial grievances. It was the

A penny for your thoughts!

voice of our country. If it were ever stolen, I'm sure it would still speak if you listened carefully."

Franklin tapped his cane on the cobblestones, stared into the distance, and briskly marched away.

"That's funny," Hunter said. "I've seen most of the re-enactors, but I've never seen that one before."

Grant turned the coin in his hand. It was crusty with dirt and the marks were impossible to see.

"Something's very strange about this," he said, perplexed.

4
WHAT'S A FUGIO?

"You're going to brush all the white off your teeth, Grant!" Christina warned as she listened to her brother brushing furiously in the bathroom of their hotel room.

"I'm not brushing my teeth!" Grant replied.

Curious, Christina skittered into the bathroom to check up on her little brother. Brown splatters dotted the mirror as Grant, tongue stuck firmly in the corner of his mouth, concentrated on his work.

"This toothpaste is working!" he said, without looking up.

Christina peered into the sink and saw that Grant was scrubbing the grimy coin Ben Franklin had given him. She also recognized the sparkly blue handle of *her* toothbrush.

"Why didn't you use your own toothbrush?" she growled.

"Forgot to bring one," he said, as if it were no big deal.

Grant rinsed the coin and stared at it. "You're not going to believe this," he said. "Better get the magnifying glass."

Christina grabbed it off her nightstand and eagerly looked at the coin. "You're right!" she told Grant. "I don't believe it. This coin was minted in 1787! Why would a historic re-enactor give you something like this? I bet it's valuable."

"Sounds like another mystery to me!" Grant said, straining to look with his sister through the magnifying glass. "Hey, what does that word, *Fugio*, mean?"

"I have no idea," Christina admitted. She did understand the words at the bottom of the coin: *Mind your business.* On the back of the curious coin were 13 linked rings. "I guess those represent the 13 original colonies," she said. In the center of the rings were the words *We Are One.*

"Grant, I think that historical re-enactor was trying to tell us something," Christina said.

"What?" Grant asked.

"Sleep on it," Christina answered. "Maybe tomorrow will bring us some answers or at least some clues."

She watched Grant climb into his bed and place the coin under his pillow. "What are you doing?" she asked.

"Sleeping on it!" Grant said.

Soon Grant was making his little-kid snoring noises. Christina tossed and turned.

Christina heard a bell. Was it the Liberty Bell? It rang over and over. Ben Franklin told her to listen to its voice. What was it telling her?

Suddenly, Christina felt a hand on her shoulder. Someone was shaking her!

5

BLACK AND WHITE AND RED ALL OVER

"Christina, wake up!" a deep voice said.

Confused, Christina rubbed her eyes and saw Papa standing by her bed.

"That must have been some dream you were having!" he said with a smile. "Didn't you hear your alarm clock ringing?"

Early morning light peeped through the curtains. "That's funny," Christina said. "I don't even remember falling asleep."

"Grant's already downstairs having breakfast with Mimi," Papa said. "Remember, today's our trip to the Pennsylvania Dutch Country." Christina frowned. "Oh, yeah," she said.

"Not interested in learning about the Amish?" Papa asked.

"It's not that," she answered. "I've just got other thoughts ringing in my head."

When Christina arrived at the hotel restaurant, Grant peeked over a tall stack of pancakes and grinned. "You snooze, you lose!" he said, as he stabbed the stack with his fork.

"What would you like for breakfast?" Mimi asked.

"I'm not feeling very hungry this morning," Christina said. "I'll just have a bowl of cereal."

Christina stretched, yawned, and finally noticed that her grandmother was dressed in white pants, a red silky blouse with a big fluffy carnation at the neck and, of course, red high heels.

"Ummm, don't you think you're overdressed for visiting the Amish?" Christina asked.

"Who knows, I might be a tourist attraction for them!" Mimi answered.

"Who are the Amish anyway?" Grant mumbled through his final forkful of pancakes.

"Grant! Don't talk with your mouth full!" Mimi scolded before answering his question. "People of several different faiths live in the Pennsylvania Dutch Country, including the Mennonites and the Amish."

"Why do they call it Dutch Country, Mimi?" Christina asked.

"These people came from Germany, which is also called Deutschland," Mimi explained. "The early colonists pronounced it 'Dutch.' William Penn, the founder of Pennsylvania and Philadelphia, promised religious freedom to those who came to this area. Penn was part of another religious group that believes in peace and equal rights for all people, the Quakers."

"A big reason people came to America was to find religious freedom," Grant said proudly. "I learned that in history this year!"

"Good for you, Grant!" Mimi said. "That's exactly right. Pennsylvania's original constitution included many rights and freedoms because of Penn. In fact, on the constitution's 50th birthday, the Pennsylvania Assembly ordered something special to celebrate it. Do you know what it was?"

Grant thought hard. "A cake with 50 candles?" he guessed.

Christina had a spoonful of cereal in her mouth when the answer came to her. "The Liberty Bell?" she said, dribbling milk out the corner of her mouth.

"Christina!" Grant said, mimicking Mimi's scolding voice.

"Right!" Mimi said.

"Getting back to your question, Grant," Mimi continued, "The Amish still live much like the early colonists did. They wear simple clothes and don't believe in using modern conveniences such as cars and phones and televisions."

"One thing's for sure," Grant said as he studied his grandmother's outfit, "you're not Amish, Mimi!"

Papa had invited Hunter and Isabella to join them, and Hunter's father dropped them off before Christina finished her cereal.

"I've got something for both of you," Hunter said, handing Christina a gift bag. Inside were two Philadelphia Phillies caps, red with a big white "P" on the front.

"We had the same idea!" Christina said. She gave both Hunter and Isabella a navy blue and red Atlanta Braves baseball cap with a white "A" on the front.

During the hour-long drive to Lancaster County, Grant pulled out the Fugio penny to show Hunter and Isabella. "What does *Fugio* mean?" Isabella asked loudly.

Christina put a finger to her mouth and softly said, *"Shhh!"* She didn't want Mimi and Papa to suspect they were already involved in a mystery.

It was too late. Mimi had heard. "I remember that word from when I took Latin in high school," she said. "It means 'I fly.'" She turned around and smiled at Isabella. "Where did you hear that word?"

Isabella smiled shyly and shrugged her shoulders.

Christina stared out the window at the open fields and crops that looked like patchwork quilts. She thought about the coin's message.

"I've got it!" she whispered to Grant. "The coin has a sundial which represents time. Time flies so mind your own business! One little mystery solved, one big mystery to go!"

Papa slowed their rental car to a crawl.

"What's going on?" Christina asked as she craned her neck to see out the windshield.

A bay horse pulling a black Amish buggy clip-clopped in front of their car. An orange triangle on the back warned motorists of a slow-moving vehicle.

Christina waved when Papa pulled around to pass. A young girl in a gray dress sat beside her father. She had golden hair which was covered with a white cap. Her father was dressed in black from head to toe. The girl waved back timidly.

As their car picked up speed, acres of sunflowers became a yellow blur. Suddenly, Mimi cried,

"STOP!"

Papa turned sharply and the tires crunched onto a gravel road. Down a long lane at a shop selling handmade Amish items, patchwork quilts fluttered on a line like colorful butterflies. "I can see this may take a while," Papa said, and winked as Mimi grabbed her purse and dashed into the store.

Inside, Grant immediately spotted clear jars filled with colorful stick candy. He plunked his money down at the counter, being careful not to include his Fugio penny.

Christina admired shiny pieces of pottery covered with sunflowers, chickens, and farm scenes.

"Would you like to see how it's made?" a young man dressed in black asked.

"Sure," Christina said, startled.

Like ducks in a row, the kids followed him to a shed. Inside, he slapped a chunk of clay onto a potter's wheel that he spun with his foot.

"It's like magic!" Grant said as the ugly lump slowly transformed into a graceful pitcher.

When the young man turned to open a fiery kiln and pull out a finished pitcher he had completed earlier, Christina noticed something red peeking from underneath a gray blanket. She couldn't resist. While his back was turned, she pulled up a corner and stole a look underneath. When he spun around, she quickly dropped the blanket and turned redder than the kiln fire.

Questions swirled in her mind. *What is a young Amish man doing with a bright red military coat?* she wondered.

6
CALL IT MACARONI!

"Turn up the air, Papa," Mimi begged as they headed back to Philadelphia. "I'm roasting like a Thanksgiving turkey!"

"Maybe it's all those quilts you have piled on your lap," Papa suggested. "We should put them in the trunk."

"No room," Mimi said. "The trunk's full of Amish baskets."

Christina and the kids giggled in the back seat. "Your grandparents are a hoot!" Hunter said.

"I feel like I spent the day back in time!" Christina said. "I'd enjoy living like the Amish. I could have a horse and chickens and I could read books all day—no worries!"

"You might want to **revise** that statement," said Papa. "You forgot the part about scooping horse poo, gathering eggs, and don't forget—no TV!"

Christina scratched her head. *"Wellllll,"* she said. "Maybe I'd better just stick with visiting the Amish!"

Isabella's long brown hair was blowing in the air conditioner's breeze. She rubbed her arms and shivered.

"Mimi, could we get one of those quilts back here?" she asked.

"I knew I needed to buy these quilts," Mimi said with a smile as she handed one back.

"Let's make a tent!" Grant suggested. In a flash, they were tucked in a cozy quilt cocoon.

Safe from her grandparents' ears, Christina told the others about the red coat.

"Maybe he's a re-enactor like our dad," Hunter suggested.

"Yeah," Grant said. "Weren't the British soldiers who fought during the Revolutionary War called Redcoats?"

"Yes," Christina said. "But I don't think an Amish man would do that. They don't believe in fighting."

Isabella, who had barely said a word since they got into the car, broke her silence. "What if he's not Amish?" she asked.

Before anyone could answer, car tires squealed and they all slid in a pile on top of Grant, like football players making a tackle.

Christina clawed her way out from under the quilt. "What happened, Papa?" she asked.

"A crazy driver!" Papa huffed. "He almost ran us off the road!"

Mimi smoothed her hair down with her fingers. "If it hadn't been for these quilts, my noggin would have been knockin' the windshield! Funny thing was, the man had on a wide-brimmed black hat like the Amish wear."

Christina looked at the others in wide-eyed amazement and thought, *Was Isabella right about the young man?*

As soon as they reached Philadelphia, Papa was ready to park the car for a while. "Let's stretch our legs at Welcome Park," he said.

Grant was a like a caged animal set free. "This looks like a big checkerboard!" he hollered, hopping on concrete squares crisscrossed with white marble slabs.

"It was made to show the city streets the way William Penn planned them," Hunter explained. "Do you know what the park name means?"

"It's welcoming us to Philadelphia," Christina said.

Hunter said, as if Christina had missed a game show question. "It was named for the ship that brought Penn and the first Quakers from England, the *Welcome.*"

"That must be William Penn," Christina said, pointing to a statue in the center of the park.

As they strolled over to it, Hunter explained the statue was a smaller copy of the Penn statue atop Philadelphia's City Hall. Isabella and Grant looked like living chess pieces as they hopped from square to square on the grid. When Mimi in her high heels and Papa in his cowboy boots joined the game, Christina and Hunter laughed hysterically.

"First one to the Penn statue wins!" Christina yelled.

Papa and Grant were hopping neck to neck until Grant tripped on his untied shoelace.

"And the old cowboy wins again," Papa shouted triumphantly.

Grant scrambled to the statue's base, tagged it, and turned to encourage Mimi, who had taken off her heels and was holding them in her hand. She managed to tie Isabella.

Grant frowned when he saw the statue up close. "So this is William Penn," he said, eyeing the wide-brimmed hat, long coat, knee breeches, boots, and the frilly shirt. "He has the same fashion taste as you, Mimi. Looks kinda sissy."

"It's not sissy, Grant," said Mimi. "Fashionable men of the 1700s dressed that way. It was called 'macaroni fashion.' British military officers even wrote a song about it. They were making fun of the Americans, or Yankees, as they called them. Anyone know it?"

Mimi sang with gusto, *"Yankee doodle went to town riding on a pony. Stuck a feather in his hat and called it macaroni!*

"The British soldiers were saying the Yankees were so dumb they thought they could be macaroni just by placing a feather in their cap," Mimi explained.

When Mimi and Papa went to look at a small replica of Penn's house, Grant had an idea. "I need a feather for my cap!" he declared, dashing off.

In a few minutes, he sashayed toward them with a large feather sticking out of the back of his Phillies cap. "Look, I'm macaroni!" he bragged.

"Wait!" Christina said. "That looks like a turkey feather. Where'd you get it?"

"On that park bench," Grant said, pointing.

"I don't think there are any turkeys in downtown Philadelphia," Christina said. "Let me see that."

She snatched the feather from his cap and was shocked to see dried ink on the end. "This is no ordinary feather," Christina said. "This is a quill and, I believe, a clue!"

7
FOUNDING PRANKSTER

"Do you hear it?" Christina whispered as she heard the faint sound of a distant bell.

"People claim they can sometimes hear a bell in the Independence Hall steeple even though there's not one there," Hunter said.

"OOOooo!" Grant said like a ghost. "That's creepy!"

"Tomorrow morning, let's head straight to Independence Hall to look for our next clue," Christina suggested. "That was where the Liberty Bell hung, so that's a good place to look."

Back in their hotel room, Christina watched Grant gingerly place the Fugio coin and quill pen under his pillow. "Sleeping on it seemed to work," he said. "Who knows what we'll find tomorrow!"

The next morning, Hunter and Isabella were anxiously waiting for them in the hotel lobby. "Stay inside Old City!" Mimi warned as they darted out the door. "We'll meet you later!"

The morning was hot and overcast and steam rose from the pavement as they walked toward Independence Hall. But when Christina saw the old red-brick building, she didn't feel hot. She looked up at the steeple where the Liberty Bell once hung and imagined hearing it ring out on July 4, 1776. Chills ran up and down her spine.

At school, George Washington, Thomas Jefferson, and the other Founding Fathers were just paintings with funny hairdos. Here, they had been living, breathing men. And Christina was walking in their footsteps at the very building where the United States was born!

The blue-faced clock on the steeple showed 8:30. Their timing was good. Only a few tourists were inside.

"Let's visit the Assembly Room," Christina said. "That's where the Declaration of Independence was signed."

Grant was leading the way when they rounded the corner. Christina heard a commotion.

KERPLUNK!

She was shocked to see her brother spread eagle on the wooden floor.

"Say!" a jolly voice said. "You'd make a fine rug! Sorta reminds me of the American eagle in the center of the rug in Congress Hall, especially since you have a feather!"

It was the same mysterious Ben Franklin they'd seen at the Ghost House. "Sorry about that, lad!" he apologized, and laughed. "Just a little prank I like to play on fellow legislators."

"I never knew you were such a prankster," Grant said, jumping to his feet and picking up the quill that had fallen from his cap. "Good one."

"That's a fine quill," Franklin said. "May I see it?"

"Sure," said Grant, "if you promise not to trip me again."

"Hmmm," Franklin hummed, writing in the air with the quill. "Reminds me of the one I used when we were drafting the Declaration of Independence in 1776. We'd had enough of the King of England telling us what to do! We wanted to be an independent country. I bet this quill would fit in that old ink stand we used."

As Franklin gave Christina a wink, she noticed the room was strangely empty of tourists. Come to think of it, every time they ran into Ben they were the only ones around. *Who is this mysterious character?* she wondered. Christina looked around the gray-green room filled with small tables covered with green cloths. Each had a quill and ink stand. Christina let her hand glide along the curved back of one of the simple, Windsor-style chairs and said, "There are a lot of ink stands in here. Which one do you mean?"

"Oh, it's not in here," Franklin said. "It's on display in the West Wing of the State House."

"Where's the State House?" Christina asked.

"Why, you're in it, dear girl," Franklin said, resting his chin on his cane. "This building was

How did people write with this thing?

completed in 1753, the same year I was appointed deputy postmaster of North America. It was the State House of Pennsylvania. It wasn't called Independence Hall until much later."

"You were a postmaster?" Grant asked, surprised.

"Yes," Franklin replied. "I got lots of experience as postmaster of Philadelphia before I was promoted. Now, don't you kids have some business to mind? Time flies, you know!"

"Right," Christina said. "Which way to the West Wing?"

Franklin pointed the way and they set off down a long hall. When Christina remembered they'd forgotten the quill, she rushed back. The quill was lying on a chair, the room was full of tourists, and Franklin was gone!

8

SITTING ON THE SUN

"There it is!" Grant shouted, when he spotted the silver inkstand among the original copies of the Declaration of Independence and the U.S. Constitution.

The park ranger in the room was busy answering a curious tourist's question. Christina saw her opportunity. The inkstand had four holes, and she plunged the quill into one. She was shocked to see a tiny scroll pop through another hole. She quickly stuffed it in her pocket and cleared her throat loudly. When the other kids looked at her, she motioned for them to follow.

Rushing back down the long hall, Christina had the strange sensation someone was following them. *Had she gotten a clue meant for someone else?*

When they reached the Assembly Room, Christina gathered the others close around her. When she was sure no one could see, she pulled the tightly rolled note from her pocket and unrolled it. It was written on parchment paper, just like the Declaration of Independence and the Constitution.

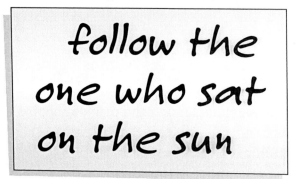

follow the
one who sat
on the sun

"Who could that be?" Christina sighed, disappointed with the clue.

Grant couldn't resist putting in his two cents' worth. "Someone with a hot backside?" he said with a snicker.

Hunter grinned. "I think I might know," he said.

Isabella nodded. "We've had several field trips here," she said. "Listen to the ranger."

The park ranger, telling the room's history, slowly made his way to the raised platform against the back wall. There, he pointed with reverence to a chair that was different from the others in the room. "This," he said, "is the chair used by George Washington during the 1787 Constitutional Convention. The sun carved into the back is rising over a new nation."

"We're supposed to follow George Washington!" Christina exclaimed.

"Isn't he dead?" Grant asked.

"Don't be silly, Grant," Christina said sternly. "We can visit some of the places linked to him around Philadelphia. Hopefully, one of them will lead us to our next clue. Ben's right. Time is flying. The Fourth of July is only two days away!"

Christina glanced around the room while slipping the note back in her pocket. Something caught her eye. *Was it a man dressed in black or just a shadow?*

9
CROSSING THE DELAWARE

The gray clouds had lifted and good-natured birds were chirping cheerfully in the trees outside Independence Hall. Christina was happy to spot Mimi and Papa.

"Did you learn everything there is to know about the birth of our nation?" Mimi asked.

"We learned a lot, but not as much as I want to know," Christina replied.

"Maybe we can help with that," Papa said. "How would all of you like to cross the Delaware just like George Washington?"

"Papa, you read my mind!" Christina said, giving him a bear hug.

An actor dressed as George Washington welcomed them aboard the strangest vehicle Grant had ever seen. On the side it said, "Ride the Ducks."

"Is this a car or a boat?" he asked.

"Both," Washington replied. "It's an amphibious vehicle—it can travel on water or land."

"Did they have these in 1776?" Grant asked, confused.

"Of course not, Grant!" Christina snapped.

Papa explained, "These vehicles were used during World War II. This one has been rebuilt to haul tourists instead of soldiers."

The odd-looking vehicle pulled into traffic, and Washington told them the story of his famous crossing.

"Those Redcoats chased my Continental Army into Pennsylvania," he said, as if his mind had drifted back several hundred years. "On Christmas night, 1776, I had to make a decision. The enlistments of many of my men were up at the end of the month. They were eager to return to their homes and families. To make matters worse, the weather was horrible, the river was choked with ice, and a cruel wind was blowing sleet and snow."

Grant whispered under his breath, "I could use a little of that ice right now! It's hot in here."

Washington continued, "it almost broke my heart to see that many of the men did not even have shoes and that they were marching through snow! I had to do something, or the British could declare victory. The revolution to make the colonies a new country free from British rule would be over."

Christina and Isabella jumped when Washington suddenly yelled, "We had to attack! We crossed the Delaware River above Trenton, New Jersey. The next morning, we attacked and won the battle. It was a turning point in the war."

Washington chuckled. "I think you know how everything turned out. If my brave men had not followed me across the Delaware, you would have a king instead of a president.

"Now," Washington continued, "are you brave enough to follow me across the Delaware?"

"YES!" they screamed with enthusiasm.

The veins in Washington's neck bulged as he shouted with authority,

"ATTACK!"

Suddenly, the vehicle pulled off the road and plunged into the river. Water droplets hit Christina like bullets, stinging her cheeks and blurring her vision.

Grant cried. "This am-fib-whatever-it-is sure is one cool ride!"

Christina blinked hard to clear the water from her sapphire blue eyes. When she opened them, she thought she was seeing things. She blinked hard again. It was still there—a wooden ship with tall white sails. It looked like it had sailed straight out of the 1700s!

"What luck!" Washington exclaimed before Christina could express her surprise. "A tall ship like the ones I used to see on the river!"

"Haven't you seen that one before?" Christina asked.

"No," Washington answered. "I don't recognize that one. It must be here for the July 4th celebration."

He turned and looked Christina straight in the eye, "It's something good to keep an eye on."

Christina wished Grant had the binoculars he was so fond of carrying. Instead he only had the magnifying glass, which would be no help reading the ship's name.

When their Delaware River cruise ended, they bid General Washington goodbye.

"Thanks for winning the war for us," Grant said, shaking Washington's hand.

"The best way to thank me," Washington replied solemnly, "is for you to do something for your country."

He was shaking Grant's hand, but Christina noticed he looked straight at her again.

Christina knew what she had to do for her country—find the Liberty Bell—but time was running out!

FREEDOM ISN'T FREE

"Since we learned some things about George Washington, we thought we'd take you all by Washington Square," Papa announced. "Does that sound OK?"

"Papa, now I *know* you're reading my mind," Christina said as she gave him another big hug.

The park was as peaceful as the river ride had been wild. The breeze in the tall trees seemed to whisper to them to come in out of the sun. Grant and Hunter were happy to listen.

"Whew!" Grant said, wiping his forehead. "A glass of lemonade would hit the spot about now."

"Come on!" Isabella said. "I'll show you the coolest place in the park."

"Go!" Mimi said. "We'll catch up with you!"

As they jogged along the gray, block path, Christina noticed several markers.

"What are these?" Christina asked. "They almost look like tombstones."

"They are," Hunter said.

Grant and Christina stopped dead in their tracks. "You're trying to scare me, right?" Christina said. "You know it's not nice to scare the tourists!"

"I'm not trying to scare you," Hunter said. "During the 1700s, this park was used as a burial ground. And during the Revolutionary War, more than 2,000 soldiers were buried here."

Grant was amazed. "You m-m-mean we're probably walking on top of d-d-dead people?" he stuttered.

"Don't worry," Hunter said. "They won't bother you."

"I still don't want to come here at night," a wide-eyed Grant said.

Isabella led them to a fountain, surrounded by a pool of water. "If you sit on the edge, you can feel the mist," she said, waving the fine spray toward her face.

"Nice!" Grant said, leaning toward the fountain.

"Grant, don't..." Christina began to caution. She was too late.

KERSPLASH!

Grant belly flopped into the pool.

"Last one in is a rotten egg!" Hunter cried, jumping in feet first.

Christina and Isabella exchanged mischievous grins and slipped in beside them. The cool water felt heavenly!

As they were splashing and giggling, Christina watched Grant's expression change from joy to terror. His body went rigid as a statue. "Fire!" he yelled. Grabbing his Phillies cap off his head, he scooped up a capful of water and jumped out of the pool.

Confused, a dripping Christina followed on his heels. Finally, she saw what her brother had seen. A flame was rising out of the concrete and behind it was a statue of George Washington!

"Halt!" A man dressed as a Revolutionary War soldier stuck his arm in front of Grant's chest. Water from his cap splashed everywhere, making a lacy pattern on the walkway.

"What do you think you're doing, lad?" the soldier asked.

"Trying to put out a fire!" Grant answered, exasperated.

"Now listen here," the soldier said. "That's one fire you never want to put out! It helps us remember and honor the men who died for our liberty. Freedom isn't free, young man!"

Christina felt sorry for Grant, whose cheeks were glowing with embarrassment. She knew he thought he was doing the right thing by putting out a fire.

Isabella quietly slipped an arm around Grant's shoulders. "It's OK, Grant," she said. "You've never been to Philadelphia before."

After the soldier walked away, Christina read the words carved in the marble wall behind the statue of Washington.

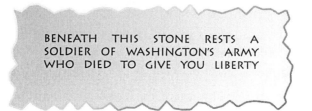

BENEATH THIS STONE RESTS A SOLDIER OF WASHINGTON'S ARMY WHO DIED TO GIVE YOU LIBERTY

"How did they decide which soldier to bury here?" Christina asked.

"This monument wasn't built until the 1950s," Hunter said. "Archaeologists came in and took a body from one of the mass graves."

"Mass graves?" she asked.

Hunter explained, "So many soldiers died in such a short period of time there wasn't time to dig individual graves. Big trenches were dug and the caskets were stacked inside."

"How sad!" Christina sighed. "I never thought much about people who died during the Revolutionary War."

"Yeah," Hunter agreed. "They said the unknown soldier was only about 20 years old."

Christina looked thoughtfully at the statue of Washington with fresh flowers and flags tucked around its base. She thought he looked determined, but sad. She looked in the direction Washington was gazing and could see the steeple of Independence Hall peeking over the tree tops. She picked up one of the little flags. "We're supposed to follow Washington, but where's he leading us?" Christina asked.

"Maybe that's your answer," Hunter said, touching the flag in Christina's hand. "Washington needed a flag for his men to follow. Where did he go for that?"

"Betsy Ross!" Christina, Grant, and Isabella said in unison.

"Her house is only a few blocks away," Hunter said. "What are we waiting for?"

The late-afternoon shadows were growing long. Christina's skin felt prickly as she dashed along with the others through the graveyard-turned park. Then, she heard it again, the faint cry of a distant bell.

To her it was saying, *Hurry! Hurry! Hurry!*

11
A STITCH IN TIME

Breathless, the kids arrived at the home of Betsy Ross. It was a narrow, two-story house with a dormer and white shutters. An iron gate opened to a small courtyard. The house was quiet and dark. The shutters of the front window were closed tight. The only movement came from a larger version of the flag Christina had picked up at Washington Park, which fluttered lazily above their heads in the dusk.

"We're too late," Christina moaned while pushing on the front door. "It's already closed."

"Why don't you knock?" Isabella suggested.

"Yeah, right," Grant teased. "You think Betsy Ross is gonna answer the door?"

Christina gave her brother a "that-was-so-rude" look and said, "Why not? It's worth a try."

She rapped softly on the white wooden door. No answer.

"Told you so," Grant said with a smirk.

The kids had already turned to walk away when a long, low

made them look back. The door had opened!

They crowded around the door's threshold and peered inside. "Come in, quickly," a soft voice whispered.

Christina pushed the door open and motioned for the others to follow. In the dim light, she saw a white cap and could hear the rustle of petticoats. Suddenly, a match flared and she could see the full figure of a woman sitting in the corner. The woman touched the match to a candle, which offered a dull glow.

"Have a seat," the woman said as she picked up a needle, pulled a red, white, and blue flag onto her lap and began stitching down a white star. She glanced at the little flag in Christina's hand and said, "George sent you, didn't he?"

Thirteen stars and thirteen stripes!

Christina was shocked. "Yes, he d-d-did," she stuttered. "Are you B-B-Betsy R-Ross?"

"Of course," the woman answered. "George came to my shop one night long ago. I believe it was 1777. He was with two other men, Robert Morris and George Ross, the uncle of my late husband. They told me our new country needed a flag—that the soldiers needed something to symbolize what they were fighting for. Business had been slow here at my upholstery shop since the war started, and I needed some work. I told them I would try.

"George gave me a sketch of a flag," she continued. "It had 13 red and white stripes and 13 six-pointed stars on a blue background."

Betsy chuckled. "I told George it would be easier to make the stars with five points, like this," she said, folding a piece of white fabric and snipping it with her scissors.

Betsy's face grew serious as she gripped a corner of the flag. "Symbols of our country are important, because they remind us of our history and bind us together."

"Like the Liberty Bell?" Christina asked.

"Yes, dear, like the Liberty Bell," she replied, smiling.

"Is there anything we should know?" Christina asked. "Anything you need to tell us?"

With that, Betsy rose from her seat and walked to a side door, motioning them to follow.

"Leave quietly through the garden gate," she cautioned. "But watch out for the Redcoats!"

The kids stumbled across uneven bricks, pushed up by the roots of a large tree, until they reached the gate. Hunter yanked it shut behind them with a clack.

Christina jumped when she felt something vibrating in her pocket. She had forgotten about her cell phone.

"Where are you?" an irritated Mimi asked when she flipped it open.

Christina slapped her forehead when she realized they had left the park without telling Mimi and Papa. "Sorry, Mimi," she said. "Our curiosity got the best of us. Since we're having supper at City Tavern, can we meet you there?"

Christina slipped the phone back in her pocket. "We'd better not be late," she warned the others. "Mimi's pretty steamed."

CLACK!

Hunter had closed the gate, but now it was open again. It was getting hard to see, but Christina swore she could see something red. And was that the

click clack

of boot heels on the sidewalk?

"Run!" Christina shouted. "Run!"

12
SWEET POTATO SURPRISE

Grant sniffed the air like a hound dog on a rabbit's trail. "Something smells *deeeelicious!*" he said, licking his lips.

If a Redcoat had been following them, they had managed to lose him and now they all had food on their minds.

Inside City Tavern, dishes clanked and servers in colonial costumes carried steaming plates of food on blue and white plates. Mimi and Papa already had a table and were bathing strange-looking biscuits in butter.

"Those are biscuits?" Christina asked.

"Mmmm, yes," Mimi said, taking a bite.

"Why are they orange?" Grant asked. "They don't look like your biscuits."

Mimi was busy chewing, so Papa answered.

"These are sweet potato biscuits," he said. "They were Thomas Jefferson's favorites."

"You mean Thomas Jefferson ate here?" Grant asked.

"All the Founding Fathers ate here," said Papa. "In fact, it was a gathering place for members of the first Continental Congress and George Washington used it as a headquarters for the Continental Army."

Christina, who had been reading the menu, which included the restaurant's history, added, "It says here the original City Tavern was torn down in 1854, but they built an almost exact replica that opened in time for our country's bicentennial."

"What's a bison ten?" Grant asked. "Aren't bison the same as buffalo?"

Hunter laughed. "Oh, no," he replied, "a bicentennial celebration is like a 200th birthday party! Our country's party was in 1976, 200 years after 1776."

A server brought their drinks in heavy pewter goblets and asked for their orders.

Papa and Mimi ordered roast duckling to share while Grant and Hunter agreed to split the braised rabbit.

"eewwww!"

Christina cried. "I could never eat a duck or a rabbit." Isabella nodded in agreement.

"Wild game is a taste you would have to **acquire**," Papa said. "But the early colonists didn't have a choice. It was often all they had."

The girls decided to share the Martha Washington turkey pot pie. Papa also ordered a bowl of West Indies pepperpot soup for them all to try.

Soon they were all stuffed. Grant ate his last bite of rabbit and declared, "Guess I better *HOP* to the bathroom before we head home!"

Hunter laughed. "I'd better go with you," he said.

Christina and Isabella waited at the table while Mimi and Papa explored the gift shop.

"How'd you like the sweet potato biscuits?" asked a tall man with gray hair pulled into a short ponytail.

Christina was startled. "You look just like Thomas Jefferson!" she exclaimed. "I've always admired the work you—I mean he—did writing the Declaration of Independence."

"Thank you!" the Jefferson look-alike said. "I don't believe in **prosaic** ideas, especially when it comes to new countries!"

The Jefferson look-alike reached inside his coat and pulled out a pocket watch. As he did, a $100 bill came out with it and fluttered to the floor.

"You dropped your money!" Christina said. She picked it up to hand it to him.

Jefferson shook his head and pushed her outstretched hand away. "No, you need this," he said. "I found it and I know you'll figure out what to do with it."

The Jefferson look-a-like snapped his pocket watch closed. "Time sure flies! I must go."

Christina stared at Ben Franklin on the bill. *Was this truly a clue from Ben or was it dropped by a careless Redcoat?*

13
MINTY FRESH CLUE

"One more day till the Fourth!" Mimi exclaimed, unfolding her newspaper to read while they waited outside the U.S. Mint for Hunter and Isabella to join them. "You kids getting excited about celebrating our country's birthday?"

"You bet," Grant said. "I can't wait to see the rockets' red glare and bombs bursting in air."

"I think you'll have to settle for fireworks," Papa chuckled.

Christina had kept quiet about the $100 bill she had deep in her pocket. If anyone saw a kid her age with that much money, they'd be suspicious for sure. If the bill was a clue, Christina didn't know what it meant.

When a yellow cab stopped in front of them, she was impressed to see Hunter and Isabella pay the driver and slide out. They didn't even have an adult with them! Would Mimi and Papa allow them to do that in Atlanta? Probably not.

As they headed into the mint, Grant said, "I'm not too crazy about mint. Do they sell any other kind of candy here?"

Christina didn't miss this chance to show her knowledge of the U.S. Mint. "They don't sell mint or any other candy here," she said. "This is where they make coins!"

"Welcome to the oldest mint in the country!" a tour guide said, and opened the door to let them inside. "As soon as you all walk through the metal detector, we'll begin our tour."

"Wow!" Grant exclaimed when they reached a room the size of a football field. Machines were everywhere, stamping coins from sheets of gold and silver metals. Each time a powerful machine stamped out coins, the floor vibrated. Shiny new coins flashed like goldfish in a crowded tank.

"You could fill a lot of piggy banks with that!" Grant said, admiring the money.

"You are looking at millions of dollars worth of coins!" the tour guide said.

Christina saw a man inspecting coins under a light with a special eyepiece. If there was a message on the $100 bill, she could surely see it with that!

"Could I inspect a coin, please?" Christina asked their guide.

He whispered to the coin inspector who seemed flattered someone was so interested in his job. He grinned and motioned for Christina to join him. She looked at a coin through the powerful magnifying piece. As the inspector chatted with the others on the tour, she slipped out the $100 bill and quickly scanned it. Sure enough, she saw a tiny message:

follow my
parkway to
my museum

CREEPY COPIES

Although they looked hurt that Christina and Grant didn't want to stay with them, Mimi and Papa agreed Hunter could take the kids exploring again.

Christina finally shared the message she found on the $100 bill and her confusion over who it was from and who it was meant for.

"Maybe someone knows we're looking for the Liberty Bell and they're trying to throw us off the trail," Isabella said.

"We have to do something, so we might as well check it out," Hunter said. "My guess is we need to take the Ben Franklin Parkway to the Museum District."

"Can we walk there?" Christina asked.

"It's too far," Hunter said, "and I already spent all my money on cab fare to get to the mint."

"No worries," said Christina, hailing a cab like she knew what she was doing. "I have plenty of money!"

When the cab stopped at a red light in front of the Mutter Museum, Grant said, "I guess there's a museum for everything—even one for people who don't talk good!"

"Speak well!" Christina corrected. She wanted to be a writer like Mimi, so she was always editing Grant's grammar.

"It's not a museum about people who mutter," Isabella said, poking Grant in the ribs. "It was named for Dr. Mutter, and I think it's the coolest museum in Philadelphia, if you're not a wimp with a weak stomach."

"You callin' me a wimp?" Grant said, trying to make muscles bulge from his scrawny arms.

"Let's see how brave you are," Isabella said, and asked the cab driver to pull to the curb.

The cab driver gave Christina a funny look when she handed him a $100 bill, but shrugged, took it with no questions, and gave her change. Grant puffed out his chest and marched like a brave soldier toward the door. His chest quickly fell flat, once inside, as he stared up at a giant skeleton in a glass case.

Everywhere Christina looked there were skulls and skeletons and grotesque organs floating in glass jars. "Is this a house of horrors?" Christina asked, crinkling her nose and frowning.

"It was started in the 1800s as a collection to educate doctors about the human body and things that can go wrong," Isabella explained.

"Something went really wrong with that guy," Grant said, pointing at the giant skeleton. "He's even too tall to be a basketball player!"

"Would you like to meet Chang and Eng?" Isabella asked.

She led them to a plaster cast of two men who were joined together at the chest.

"They're the reason twins who are joined together are called Siamese twins!" Christina read from the information. "They were from the country of Siam." Her mind was working fast. "So this is just a hollow copy of the real thing..."

Hunter seemed to be thinking hard, too. "Yeah," he said slowly. "If you poured something inside, like melted metal, it would make a copy."

"Interesting," Christina said. "That would be the same way someone would make a copy of the Liberty Bell!"

15
THE BRITISH ARE COMING!

Christina was glad Isabella suggested a quick side trip to the Mutter Museum, but their next clue was probably waiting at the Franklin Institute.

"We could walk from here," Hunter said.

"Let's run," Christina suggested.

Soon, they approached a large fountain in Logan Square with sprays of water shooting skyward like geysers. Children splashed and shouted in the shallow pool surrounding it.

"That looks so cool!" Grant said, panting from the heat. "I'm so hot, you could fry an egg on my head!"

"That's the Swann Memorial Fountain," said Hunter. "It has three statues in it that represent Philadelphia's three main waterways."

"We have to mind our manners, Grant," Christina said, glancing back to give him a look that said, *Get in that fountain and I'll tell Mimi how that big spot got on her sofa!*

But when Christina looked behind her she was no longer worried about Grant. She saw men in red coats jogging toward them. Remembering Betsy's warning, she told Hunter, "We need to hide—fast!"

"Follow me," Hunter said. They cut through Logan's Square, zigzagging through trees and hedges.

Christina imagined she heard an entire army on their heels. *Or is it just my heart pounding,* she wondered, afraid to look back. Unable to run any farther, the kids collapsed in a heap on velvety grass.

"We did it!" Hunter said between heaving breaths. "I don't see Redcoats anywhere!"

When he had caught his breath, Grant noticed the nearby statue of a boxer with arms held high in victory. "I don't know who that guy is, but I know how he feels!" he said.

"Haven't you ever seen the movie *Rocky?*" Hunter asked.

"Have we seen that?" Grant asked Christina. "I think that's the one we watched with Papa a few months ago. He said it was one of his favorites, but he started snoring before it was over."

"It was filmed here in Philly," Hunter said. "And the famous scene of Rocky running up the steps took place here at the Philadelphia Museum of Art."

He pointed to a building that resembled a Greek temple. A mountain of marble steps led to it. Hunter continued, "Most tourists who come to Philly have to run up those steps before they leave town and do a victory dance like Rocky."

"Gotta do it!" Grant said, scrambling to his feet.

"We'll provide the music," Isabella said. She began to sing the movie theme, *Gonna fly now—Da Da Daaaaa, Da Da Daaaa...*

Grant dashed up the steps like a boxer in training. When he reached the top, he raised his arms in victory and danced a jig.

Christina noticed that angry, black clouds were gathering in the sky above them. Distant lightning danced across the horizon. And was it her imagination, or was she hearing bells again?

16
LIGHTNING BELLS

Christina pinched her shirt and flapped it away from her body. Her skin felt sticky. The hot air had grown muggy from the approaching storm when they reached the Franklin Institute Science Museum.

Inside, bells chimed like a frantic alarm. Christina didn't know how she had heard them from so far away. A 21-foot-tall marble statue of Benjamin Franklin welcomed them. Founded in 1824, the museum had been opened to honor the man who had made so many scientific discoveries, including that famous experiment with electricity! When Christina looked into the stone face, she felt it was telling her she was on the right track.

Grant's eyes lit up like Christmas morning when he saw all the cool science displays. After history, science was his favorite subject. There was even a giant model of a heart for visitors to walk through! With time quickly running out, Christina knew they needed to focus on their mission.

"Maybe we can come back to visit when we aren't in a hurry," she promised Grant.

The kids followed the ringing sound to Electricity Hall. Grant and Hunter stopped at a display that showed how Franklin used a kite and a key to prove that lightning is a form of electricity.

Christina and Isabella found what they were looking for at a display called Franklin's Bells. "Static electricity makes them ring when a storm's approaching," Christina read.

Grant, who had joined them, said, "So that's how he knew when to go outside and fly his kite! These bells are going crazy. That must be a doozy of a storm coming."

Christina looked all around the display for strange lettering, a sticky note, anything that might say "clue." Nothing.

"There has to be another clue somewhere in this museum," she said.

"Look over there," Isabella whispered and hid her pointing finger with her other hand. A man was untying the kite string in the lightning display.

He wore a long trench coat and was not wearing a name tag like the other museum employees. He slipped the key into his coat pocket and tied another key onto the string.

"He's changing the key!" Christina said with a gasp.

When the man spun around, his coat flared and revealed something underneath. Something red!

Grant slapped his hand over his mouth to keep from blurting out, "It's one of them!"

"I bet that key was part of a clue," Christina sighed. "Guess we'll never know now."

Grant flashed a sly smile and pulled a plastic case out of his pocket. "Maybe we will," he said. Inside the case was the plastic putty Grant loved to play with. And in the putty was an impression of a key!

Christina planted a big kiss on her little brother's cheek. "Grant, you're a genius," she said. "A regular Sherlock Holmes!"

Grant wiped the kiss off his cheek, but grinned proudly.

Leaving the museum, Christina patted the cold stone of Franklin's statue. She looked up and could see something stuck to the underside of his hand. Without thinking, she scurried up high enough to reach it. She pulled out a small parchment scroll stuck between the massive fingers. Safely on the floor, she read it to the others:

when Jefferson checks the time,
the lock will be locked

17
GHOSTLY POSTMAN

Outside, the weather was changing faster than a **chameleon** changes colors. The kids squinted to shield their eyes from grit the hot wind swept off the sidewalks. Christina was shocked to see how low the sun was when it peeked between the black, ominous clouds. No wonder her stomach was rumbling. She hadn't eaten since breakfast!

"My stomach's roaring louder than a lion!" Grant said, as if he had read Christina's mind.

"Mimi and Papa are probably getting worried about us," said Christina, reaching into her pocket for her cell phone. "I'm surprised Mimi hasn't called already."

When Christina's hand came out empty, she started to frantically pat her other pockets. No cell phone. "Oh yeah!" she said, remembering. "I gave it to Mimi when I walked through the metal detector at the mint. I forgot to get it back from her. How could I be so **neglectful**?"

"We were supposed to meet them to take the ghost tour," Hunter said. "Let's take a cab to Society Hill, where it starts."

"Just don't forget we have another clue to unravel," Christina reminded them. "We only have hours to solve this mystery, not days."

Even in the dusky light, Christina could see that Society Hill, filled with old homes from the 1600s and 1700s, was a beautiful section of Philadelphia.

Hunter told them Society Hill got its name from the Free Society of Traders that William Penn had started to help grow the new town of Philadelphia. Years later, after the Revolutionary War, it had been home to many powerful men who played important roles in the new federal government.

The cab dropped them off at Christ Church. Its red brick looked ancient, but its white steeple proudly still pointed to the heavens.

"My grandmother goes to church here," Isabella said. "She told me it was started in 1695, but this building was built in 1744. Many of the Founding Fathers worshipped here—even George Washington and Benjamin Franklin!"

Christina looked up and down the cobblestone streets. There was no sign of Mimi and Papa and no sign of a ghost tour.

"It was probably canceled because of the weather," said Christina, brushing her wind-blown hair out of her face. That was when she saw something fluttering against the church's iron gate.

Probably just a piece of trash, she thought. Christina picked it up, but the dark sky made it impossible to read. She scurried to a street lamp that was just blinking on.

What she thought might be trash was an envelope made of parchment. She turned it over and saw an odd stamp. When she saw the postmark, she almost fainted. It said 1776! *Was it another message from their old friend Ben, who had been a postmaster?* With trembling fingers, she opened it and pulled out a note:

liberty could leave the
same way it came

18
LIGHTS OF LIBERTY

"First, men in red coats are after us and now UFOs!" Grant hollered between loud claps of thunder. He was staring at strange lights wildly dancing off the cloud bottoms. "Maybe a UFO stole the Liberty Bell. Probably beamed it right up!"

Hunter laughed at Grant's imagination. "You've been watching too much science fiction," he said. "I bet that's the Historic Lights of Liberty—not a UFO."

"What are the Historic Lights of Liberty?" Christina asked, not quite sure whether she should run or stay put.

"It's a special history presentation for kids," Hunter answered. "Pictures flashed onto Independence Hall and other historic buildings tell the story of the birth of our nation."

"Does it include Jefferson?" Christina asked, trying to piece together clues like a puzzle.

"Yes," Hunter said.

Christina's face lit up like the sky on the Fourth of July. "And isn't there a clock on Independence Hall?"

Hunter knew where Christina was going. "When Jefferson checks the clock!" he said. "The lock will be locked!"

Christina's face fell. "Too bad we don't know what lock will be locked."

Lightning exploded in the sky and flashed creepy shadows on the church's front wall.

"Let's figure it out on the way," Isabella said with a quivering voice.

Despite the bad weather, a large crowd had gathered at Independence Hall.

"I'm sure Mimi and Papa are in this crowd somewhere," Grant said, hopping up and down to try to get a better look. "Wish I was as tall as that skeleton we saw, so I could find them."

The *rat-a-tat-tat* of drums and the boom of cannon fire from the history presentation mingled with the rumble of thunder. On the front of Independence Hall, scenes of the struggle for independence flashed.

"This is awesome!" Christina told Hunter and Isabella. She wanted to see if Grant was as impressed with the display as she was, but he was nowhere to be seen.

"He's off looking for Mimi and Papa, I guess," Christina said.

Isabella's mouth fell open in shock. "Well, I guess he's got the best view possible!"

Christina looked. Far above them, in the steeple of Independence Hall, was Grant! He waved and said something Christina couldn't hear. She motioned for him to come down.

Suddenly, lightning peeled through the sky, crackling with electricity. Sparks flew from the top of the steeple. The flash made spots dance across Christina's eyes. When they were finally clear, she looked back at the tower. Grant was gone!

Christina was frantic. "The Redcoats probably nabbed him!" she cried.

"BOO!"

a voice said.

Christina almost jumped out of her skin. Then, she realized it was her little brother standing safely beside her.

"How cool was that!" Grant said. "Sometimes it pays to be small and sneaky! Nobody even noticed me."

"You scared the stuffin' outta me!" Christina wailed, grabbing her chest in relief. "Did you see Mimi and Papa?"

"No, but you can see everything from up there," Grant replied. "It helped me figure out that last clue. How did the Liberty Bell come to America?"

"By boat," Hunter answered.

"Didn't the clue say Liberty could leave the same way it came? I think it was talking about the Liberty Bell leaving America on a boat. From the steeple, I saw the sails of that big old boat we saw on the Delaware River."

Hunter had a worried look on his face. "Usually they fold those sails at night..." he said.

"...unless they're in a hurry to sneak away!" Christina finished his sentence.

"The boat was docked at Penn's Landing," Hunter said.

"Wait!" Isabella shouted. She was looking at Independence Hall again. "We may be too late!"

The image of Jefferson was looking at the clock on the bell tower—it was 8:30.

"The lock is locked!" Christina cried. "The Liberty Bell is locked up on that ship somewhere and it's time to set sail. We have to board that ship!"

19
FOR WHOM THE BELL TOLLS

The water at Penn's Landing was choppy from the storm. The old wooden boat creaked and groaned as it bobbed up and down. White sails, as big as the sheets on a giant's bed, flapped impatiently.

The kids crouched behind an ice cream stand and watched. Christina was not surprised to see about a dozen men in red coats crawling around the boat like red ants.

BOOOOM!

The loudest clap of thunder yet shook the earth beneath their feet. The light mist turned into blowing, stinging raindrops. Above the noise,

Christina could hear the faint, but steady sound of a bell.

DONG!

DONG!

DONG!

"It's now or never!" Christina yelled, darting across the slippery concrete toward the pier.

The wooden plank leading from the pier to the ship was even slicker. Christina eased across it gingerly, keeping a careful eye on the water churning far below. Grant wobbled on the plank and almost fell. Hunter grabbed his arm and steadied him. So far, so good. The Redcoats were so busy that they hadn't seen the kids.

"Follow the sound," Christina mouthed, pointing to her ears. On tip toes, they reached a door. It was unlocked! They eased into a cramped stair landing. It felt wonderful to get out of the pounding rain!

"Listen!" Christina whispered. The bell sounds were coming from below. "Down these stairs!" she ordered, leading the way.

The ship's hold smelled musty. The only light came from a small lantern swaying from the ceiling.

The bell tones were stronger now. Christina followed her ears.

"Over here!" she cried. Christina pointed to a huge wooden crate wrapped with a heavy chain that was secured with a padlock as big as a plate.

She heard footsteps on the stairs. A Redcoat was coming! The kids cowered beside the crate.

"Stop that tapping!" a gruff voice hollered. "Nobody can hear you. You're going back to England with us!"

The Redcoat headed straight for the crate!

"Quiet!" he yelled again.

The kids were surprised to hear a muffled voice reply from inside the crate, "The voice of liberty will never be silenced!"

The Redcoat gave a wicked laugh and slammed a ring of keys on top of the crate. "When you decide to get quiet, I'll come back and give you a drink of water." He laughed again and creaked back up the stairs.

Christina couldn't believe their luck. She grabbed the keys and tapped the crate. "Hold on!" she said. "We'll have you out in a jiffy!"

"Hurry!" the voice inside said. "The ship will set sail any minute!"

Christina fumbled with the keys. There must have been 50 of them on the ring. "I'll never find the right one!" she fretted.

"Wait!" Grant said. "I have a copy, remember?" He pulled out his plastic putty case with the impression of the key from the Franklin Institute. It was a skeleton key with a heart at the top.

"Got it!" Christina said, finding the key on the ring with the same shape. She quickly opened the lock and the four of them removed the heavy chain and opened the crate.

The children gasped. Inside were the Liberty Bell—and a young man dressed in black. It was the potter from the Amish shop! He crawled out slowly.

"Thank you kindly," he said. "I thought this boat ride would end at the bottom of the sea!"

Before they could ask questions, the door at the top of the stairs burst open and the Redcoat bounded down the stairs. There was no time to hide.

"I see we've got some little rats in the hold!" he bellowed. "I'll get rid of you when we get to sea!"

"SCATTER!" Christina yelled. She dove into the crate beside the Liberty Bell. It was almost as tall as her! With her heart pounding, she rubbed her hands along the cool metal. Her fingers found the letters P-E-N-S-Y-L-V-A-N-I-A. There was only one "N" at the beginning. This one was real!

Suddenly, the ship lurched to one side and Christina heard a commotion as the Redcoat lost his footing and slid across the hold.

"Charge!" she heard Grant yell. They all followed as he led the way up the stairs and onto the ship's deck where they were met by a passel of police. Close on their heels were a drenched Mimi and Papa.

Would they be grounded for life or get a medal for saving the Liberty Bell? Christina wasn't sure, but she did know there was lots of explaining to do!

20
HOT OFF THE GRILL

The kids gobbled grilled chicken fingers like they hadn't eaten in days, or at least in almost 24 hours. Right now, Christina felt like she was being grilled more than the chicken had been.

"How did you know that wasn't the real Liberty Bell in Liberty Center?" Mimi asked.

Christina explained about the "Ns."

As soon as she finished, Papa had a question about the young Amish man.

"He's a potter at the shop we visited in Amish country," she explained. "The Redcoats paid him to make a mold they could use to create a replica of the Liberty Bell. He thought he was doing something good for a group of historic re-enactors. They even gave him a red coat to make him an honorary member. Once he discovered what they were really up to, he was going to turn them in, so they locked him in the crate."

A police captain, who had interviewed several of the Redcoats, stopped by to fill in the blanks. He said the culprits were taking the famous bell back to England to hold it for ransom. Their leader was a park ranger who had been fired. He wanted revenge and lots of money and he knew the Liberty Center security system well enough to pull it off.

"I just don't understand how you kids managed to find it," the police captain said.

Christina smiled. "I guess you could say we had a lot of help from Ben and his friends."

21
IT'S GREAT TO BE FREE!

Christina yawned as they strolled to the Liberty Bell Center in the bright sunshine. It was a beautiful Independence Day.

Park personnel had worked all night to get the original Liberty Bell back in place. Right on schedule, Hunter's neighbor, Mr. Whiddon, tapped the Liberty Bell with his fingers 13 times for the 13 original colonies and in honor of his fellow soldiers who died during World War II.

Christina was glad Mimi and Papa hadn't grounded them for life. Even if they had, it would have been worth it to see the great symbol of freedom back where it belonged.

Food, fun, and fireworks would fill the rest of the day. But there was something Christina had to do. At Christ Church Burial Ground, she found the grave of Ben Franklin.

"Thanks for everything, Ben," Christina said. She tossed a penny on his grave—a custom in Philadelphia that is supposed to bring good luck.

Grant fished in his pocket for the Fugio coin. It was gone!

"Nothing here but a plain old penny and some lint," Grant whined.

"Maybe Ben was just letting you borrow it!" Christina suggested.

Mr. Whiddon, who had tagged along, watched them quietly. "The Liberty Bell is an important symbol and I'm glad you all found it," he said. "Just remember that if liberty is in your heart, no one can take it from you!"

Christina thought about their adventure. They had experienced some unusual encounters with historic characters. Christina still wasn't sure if they were re-enactors or helpful ghosts. Either way, she had a new appreciation for what had taken place so that she could grow up free in the greatest nation on Earth.

Grant expressed his feelings simply. "It's great to be free!"

Christina grinned at Mimi and Papa. "That's right, Grant," she said. "Free to solve more mysteries!"

Now...go to

www.carolemarshmysteries.com
and...

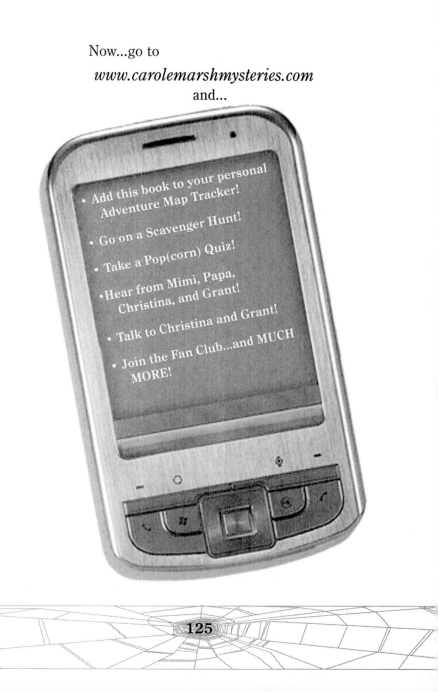

- Add this book to your personal Adventure Map Tracker!

- Go on a Scavenger Hunt!

- Take a Pop(corn) Quiz!

- Hear from Mimi, Papa, Christina, and Grant!

- Talk to Christina and Grant!

- Join the Fan Club...and MUCH MORE!

GLOSSARY

amphibious: capable of functioning on land or in water

dormer: a framed window unit projecting through a sloping roof

enlistments: those who enter the armed forces voluntarily

liberty: freedom from unjust governmental control

meandering: winding and turning

muffled: the deadened sound of something

re-enactor: a person who participates in recreating an historical event

SAT GLOSSARY

acquire: to get as one's own

chameleon: changeable in appearance

neglectful: exhibiting or indicating omission

prosaic: unimaginative

revise: to examine for the correction of errors, or for the purpose of making changes

Liberty Bell Trivia

1. The Liberty Bell first got its nickname when abolitionists, people who wanted to end slavery, used it as a symbol.

2. Before the Liberty Bell got its nickname, it was simply called the State House Bell.

3. In 1772, people who lived near the Philadelphia State House (Independence Hall) sent a petition to the Assembly that they were distressed by the constant "ringing of the great Bell in the steeple."

4. From 1790 through 1800, the Liberty Bell called voters to hand in their ballots at the State House Window.

5. The Liberty Bell weighed 2,080 pounds when it was cast.

6. The Liberty Bell's famous zig-zag crack occurred when it was rung for George Washington's birthday in February 1846.

7. More than 1.5 million people visit the Liberty Bell each year.

8. George Washington's silver household goods provided the metal for the first coins struck at the U.S. Mint in Philadelphia.

9. The U.S. Mint in Philadelphia can produce 1.8 million coins per hour.

10. In the 1700s, most men wore wigs. Lawyers and merchants wore gray wigs, tradesmen wore brown wigs, and judges and military officers wore white wigs. Those who didn't have a white wig for formal occasions made them white with flour or talcum powder.

Enjoy this exciting excerpt from:

THE MISSION POSSIBLE MYSTERY AT Space Center Houston

1 COUNTDOWN CONFUSION

Christina tried to wiggle, but the seat belt held her tighter than her grandmother's hugs. Instead, she focused on the colorful blinking lights of the console before her.

"There's no backing out now," she mumbled. Biting the corner of her lip, she feared that this time her curiosity had gotten her in over her head.

A deep voice startled her. "TEN. NINE. EIGHT. SEVEN. WE HAVE A GO FOR MAIN ENGINE START..."

Colossal engines roared to life and Christina's fingertips dug into the arms of her seat as it began to vibrate.

"SIX. FIVE. FOUR. THREE. TWO. ONE. ZERO. WE HAVE BOOSTER IGNITION AND LIFTOFF OF THE SPACE SHUTTLE EXPLORER!"

The shuttle broke free from the launch pad like a wild bull breaking out of a rodeo chute. And Christina was its rider! Every bone in her body *sh-sh*-shook and her teeth *ch-ch*-chattered.

"HOUSTON NOW CONTROLLING THE FLIGHT OF SPACE SHUTTLE EXPLORER..." the voice said. "WE HAVE NEW RESIDENTS HEADED FOR THE INTERNATIONAL SPACE STATION..."

Christina had always wondered how astronauts felt when they launched into space for the first time. Now she knew. It was scary, but exciting!

She tried to turn her head to see how her younger brother Grant and her grandparents Mimi and Papa were handling their own fear and excitement, but the powerful force of shooting into space kept her pinned firmly to her seat. Her cheeks felt like pancakes.

Christina had traveled the world with her brother and grandparents, but she never dreamed this trip would be so *out of this world!*

"SHUTTLE COMPLETING ITS ROLL FOR THE EIGHT AND A HALF MINUTE RIDE TO ORBIT," the voice announced as Christina's stomach

then

"THREE LIQUID FUEL MAIN ENGINES NOW THROTTLING BACK TO REDUCE THE STRESS ON THE SHUTTLE AS IT BREAKS THROUGH THE SOUND BARRIER..."

Christina couldn't believe her ears. She was traveling faster than sound! Her numb fingers slowly relaxed their grip as the shuttle ride became smooth—almost as smooth as cruising down the interstate in Mimi's and Papa's little red convertible.

"SHUTTLE, THIS IS HOUSTON, GO AT THROTTLE UP..." the voice said.

For the first time, Christina heard the shuttle commander's reply. "Go at throttle up," he answered.

The voice continued, "SHUTTLE ALREADY ELEVEN AND A HALF MILES IN ALTITUDE, EIGHT MILES DOWN RANGE FROM THE KENNEDY SPACE CENTER...SHUTTLE TRAVELING ALMOST 2,400 MILES PER HOUR...STANDING BY FOR SOLID ROCKET BOOSTER SEPARATION..."

A blinding

filled the windows and the shuttle lurched like a car hitting a speed bump as the rocket boosters separated and fell back to Earth.

The shuttle commander spoke again. "Congratulations! We are at 50 nautical miles and you are now officially astronauts!"

The brilliant blue sky was turning black as night. The squeezing force slowly released her, and Christina felt her arms get lighter and lighter until they floated.

"The space shuttle is now 214 miles above the South Pacific Ocean—next stop, International Space Station," the shuttle commander announced.

Suddenly, Christina wondered if the shuttle had brakes. "Will we slow down in time?" she worried. "Or will we have a space fender-bender?!"

2
MISSING MOON

"The shuttle is now traveling 17,000 miles per hour. Prepare to dock International Space Station..." the commander announced.

Christina braced herself for an explosive collision. Instead, she heard a loud CLANK and CLICK.

"Docking is complete," the commander said. "Welcome to the International Space Station, astronauts!"

SWISH!

Doors flew open. People unbuckled their seatbelts. A firm tap on her shoulder made Christina jump.

"Snap out of it!" Papa said. "The simulation ride is over."

Grant pushed past her seat. "That was awesome!" he said. "Now I understand what a simulation ride is. It makes you feel like you're really there!"

The simulation was so real to Christina that she found it difficult to return to reality. She wished she was really on the Space Station.

"Was the simulation as exciting as you imagined it would be?" Mimi asked, wrapping an arm around her starry-eyed granddaughter's trembling shoulders.

"More exciting!" Christina said as they exited the Blast Off Theater at Space Center Houston, the official visitor's center of the Johnson Space Center in Houston, Texas. "I could see myself becoming an astronaut!"

"I remember that feeling," Mimi said. "There was nothing like eating dinner on a TV tray and watching snowy pictures of Neil Armstrong take those first steps on the moon."

Grant looked confused. "I think your memory's bad about the snow," he said. "There's no snow on the moon."

"Of course not," Mimi replied. "I meant that the black and white TV picture wasn't good so it looked like snow. Technology wasn't as advanced then. We couldn't get crystal clear pictures from space like we do now."

Papa helped Mimi with the history lesson. "President John F. Kennedy said in 1961 that he wanted the United States to put a man on the moon by the end of the decade. Neil Armstrong became the first human to set foot on the moon after he and Buzz Aldrin landed the *Apollo 11* there in 1969."

"Oh!" Christina said excitedly. "Was he the guy who said, 'One small step for man; one giant leap for mankind?'"

"That's right, Christina!" Mimi exclaimed. "And don't forget it was a group of NASA scientists and engineers right here at Johnson Space Center who helped those men reach the moon. That's why they call it the 'home of human space flight.'"

"What does NASA mean?" Grant asked.

"NASA stands for National Aeronautics and Space Administration," Christina explained, proud that she knew more than her little brother. "Did you want to be an astronaut?" she asked Mimi.

"No," Mimi said. "But I was so impressed with the images of the moon and space that I wanted to be an astronomer."

"That's funny!" Grant said with a giggle. "You wanted to be an astronomer and you became a mystery writer."

"At least I can write about space," Mimi said. "Who knows? I might write a space mystery after this visit!"

Christina's eyes roamed the cavernous Space Center with all its exhibits and activities. She didn't know what to look at first.

This was a visit Christina and Grant had anticipated for months. When an old friend Judy and her husband Kent invited Mimi and Papa to visit their Houston ranch, Mimi eagerly accepted. There was no way she could **oppose** her grandkids, who begged to come along and learn about space exploration.

"You're out of this world!" Christina joked when Mimi finally said OK.

The always impatient Grant spotted something that snatched his attention. "What are those rocks doing here?" he asked.

"I'll bet those are moon rocks!" Papa said, racing Grant to the display.

Grant rubbed his fingers across a piece of gray rock as rough as the sandpaper in Papa's toolbox. "I have touched the moon!" he shouted triumphantly.

Other rocks reclined like creepy alien lumps in a long glass case. Attached to holes in the side were black rubber gloves.

"What are those gloves for?" asked Grant.

"To take the rocks in and out," Mimi answered. "Those rocks are very valuable."

"It says here that only 840 pounds of rocks have been brought back from the moon," Christina read.

"When moon rocks were first brought back to Earth, people were afraid they might contain dangerous germs," said Papa.

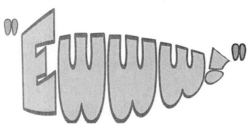

"Ewww!"

"No wonder you need to wear gloves!" Grant said, wiping his hands on his pants like they were crawling with moon cooties. "Gross!"

"Don't worry," Mimi said, laughing. "Scientists never found any germs."

Christina found one rock particularly interesting. About the size of a lumpy softball, it was a lava rock from a volcanic eruption. In 1971, *Apollo 15* astronauts collected it near the crest of Dune Crater. Somehow, it looked familiar.

"Hey Grant, this looks just like your nose," she said and laughed. "There's even a booger coming out!"

"Ha, ha," Grant said, rolling his eyes. "You're very scientific. I'm going to look at space suits."

Christina followed Grant into the Astronaut Gallery where photos of every astronaut who had flown in space lined the walls. Space movie theme songs poured from speakers and inspired Grant to become Hero Spaceman. With one fist on his hip and the other aimed for the stars, he shouted, "To infinity and beyond!"

What are those rocks doing here?

Large glass tubes held spacesuits that stood at attention as if waiting for their next mission. Some were silver, but most were white and puffy.

"They look like marshmallow men!" Christina observed.

"Are there astronauts inside these?" Grant asked, with a puzzled expression.

It was Christina's turn to roll her eyes. "Grant, can't you imagine astronauts have better things to do than stand around on display?" she asked.

"Then why did this one just *m-m-*move?" Grant asked with a quivering voice.

"You're just spacey, Grant," Christina said, moving down the line to admire a suit with a gold face shield as shiny as a mirror. She noticed her hair sticking up and was about to smooth it down when the face shield reflected a gang of security guards galloping by.

"What's going on?" she asked a young boy standing beside her.

"Someone said one of the moon rocks has been stolen!" he whispered.

Enjoy this exciting excerpt from

THE BREATHTAKING MYSTERY ON Mt. Everest THE TOP OF THE WORLD

1 SCURRYING SKIVVIES

SCREEEECH! Christina woke up with a start. Tires squealed with urgency in front of her grandparents' house. She threw back her covers and dashed to the window. Flinging back the curtains, all she could see was the flash of a silver bumper disappearing in a black cloud of exhaust fumes and burning rubber. The family dog, Clue, barked ferociously.

She watched Mimi, Papa, and Uncle Mike scurry across the yard to look at the still-smoking tire marks on the pavement. Christina rushed out to join them. Her bare feet left dark footprints in the dew-soaked grass.

"What's going on?" Christina asked.

"Don't know," Papa answered in a deep, raspy voice that told her he hadn't had his first cup of coffee. "Guess somebody was in a big hurry, or at least Clue helped them get in a big hurry."

"That a boy, Clue," Christina said, patting the bloodhound's head. "Think it could've been that teenager down the street?"

Mimi laughed. "Not at this time of the morning!" she said. "Most teenagers don't get up before noon on Saturday!"

"Oh, yeah!" exclaimed Christina excitedly. "For a second I forgot that it's Saturday—the day we're leaving for the biggest adventure of our lives!"

"You said it!" Uncle Mike agreed. "This is the day I've been dreaming of for the past two years!"

Christina could see his van in the driveway stuffed with bags and bags of gear and equipment.   She shivered with excitement. Christina had traveled all over the United States and much of the world with her little brother Grant, grandfather Papa, and grandmother Mimi, better known to many as mystery writer Carole Marsh.   Every place they went was always fascinating with lots of interesting things to see and learn, but this trip was different.   This was not a typical place tourists would choose.   Most wouldn't have the courage to go to a place so cold, isolated, and deadly!

Christina smiled proudly at her tall, handsome uncle, Mimi's only son.   He and his friend Dave had lifted weights, climbed more rock walls than a gecko, and run for miles and miles to prepare.   Now they were ready to climb the tallest mountain in the world—Mount Everest!

"HOW   EMBARRASSING!"   someone yelled from the front porch.   They all turned at once and saw that it was Grant.

"Why are you all standing out here in your skivvies?" he asked.

Christina, Papa, and Mimi exchanged looks and burst into laughter.   They suddenly realized that in the excitement of the moment, they had rushed out without even grabbing a robe. Only Uncle Mike, who had just arrived when the commotion took place, was fully dressed. Papa had pulled on his cowboy boots. But the only other thing he was wearing was his sleeping shorts covered in red airplanes that looked a lot like his own little red and white plane, *Mystery Girl.*

Mimi's short blond hair had not seen a comb yet and looked like a bird's nest on top of her head. She was wearing a long beige gown with red sequined hearts around the neck.

Christina shivered again, this time from the cool breeze. Her favorite jammies, covered with running horses, were not made for romping outside on a chilly spring morning.

"Brrrrr," Christina said through chattering teeth. "I sure could use a cup of your hot chocolate, Mimi!"

Grant waved frantically for them to come inside. Christina skittered across the grass, trying to step back into the footprints she had made on the way out. On her right she could see the jumble of footprints made by Uncle Mike,

Mimi, Papa, and Clue. But on her left, Christina noticed other marks on the grass that were not shaped like feet at all.   A curious line of triangles pointed toward the line of shrubs in front of the porch. Christina let her eyes follow the trail until she saw it.   Something was sparkling in one of the shrubs!

2
ICY OMEN

Christina was no stranger to mystery. During every trip with her grandparents, a tangled web of mystery often caught her and Grant the way a spider catches buzzing flies. She wouldn't be surprised to find a mystery waiting for them at Mount Everest, but she was surprised by a mystery beginning before they even left their home in Peachtree City, Georgia!

"Pssst!" Christina called to Grant as he was about to follow the adults inside.

She reached into the shrubs and pulled out a black envelope with gold metallic writing on it, and jumped up on the porch.

"What's that?" Grant asked, peering at the strange note.

"Whoever took off in such a hurry this morning must have delivered it," answered Christina. She traced her fingers over writing that looked like none she had ever seen. "I don't see how the note could be meant for any of us," she said. "It's not written in English!"

Christina ran her finger under the flap and opened the envelope like something inside might bite her. Gingerly she pulled out a note on thick black paper. Several slivers of ice fell out and shattered on the porch floor in a spray of sparkling crystals. Squiggly writing in the same gold ink looked like it was hanging upside down from the lines that stretched across the page. It was beautiful, but mysterious. At the bottom was a drawing of a pair of eyes and a nose that looked like a question mark.

"Who sends a letter on black paper in a black envelope with ice inside?" Grant asked. "Seems sort of creepy. Don't you think you should show it to the adults?"

"No, Grant," Christina answered. "Uncle Mike and Dave have enough worries about their climb—like staying alive! I don't want to give them anything else to worry about."

In the kitchen, Mimi watched colorful cups of hot chocolate spin in the microwave like a carousel. Papa sipped his coffee and asked, "Are you kids ready to fly to the other side of the world?"

"All packed!" Christina said proudly.

"And I have plenty of games," Grant quickly added.

Mimi plunked their hot chocolate down in front of them. "You understand this is probably the longest flight you've ever taken," she said.

"How long will it take us to get there and land on Mount Everest?" Grant asked.

Christina giggled. "Oh, Grant," she said. "You don't land on Mount Everest!"

"Yeah," Uncle Mike said. "If you could simply fly a plane to the top and land, what would be the purpose of us climbing it?"

"Right," said Grant, nodding. "Then where do we land?"

Papa pulled a small globe from a shelf and spun it around. He stopped it with his thick finger. "This is India," he said, "and this is China. We are flying into Nepal, this little sliver of country in between."

"Wow!" Grant said. "It doesn't look big enough to land a plane in!"

Papa laughed loudly. "It's larger than it looks on the globe," he said. "I promise! It's about the same size as Florida. You kids are lucky to get to visit Nepal. When I was a kid, the country was closed to visitors. It wasn't opened until 1951. Two years later something very exciting happened."

"I know!" Christina cried. "In 1953, Sir Edmund Hillary reached the summit of Mount Everest!"

Uncle Mike's friend Dave bounded into the kitchen wearing an excited grin. "Everybody got your crampons packed?" he asked.

"I don't think so," Grant said, concerned. "What are crampons?"

"They're spikes that you strap to your boots so you can climb on ice and packed snow," Dave answered.

Mimi laughed. "My high heels can do that!"

Christina chuckled at Mimi, but couldn't help but worry about the ominous black note. *What did it mean? Was it a warning?*